Logistics **mike mcneil** *sounding board* Layn just *production* **vince sneed**

All characters, stories, and art are © and ™ 2002 by Carla Speed McNeil, Any references to other work will be attributed in the notes following the story. All rights reserved. No part of this book may be reproduced by any means without the permission of Carla Speed McNeil, except for review purposes. The stories, characters, and incidents depicted within are purely fictional. Published by Lightspeed Press P.O. Box 448 Annapolis Junction, MD 20701. www.lightspeedpress.com Printed in the USA, bound in Canada. ISBN 0-9673691-3-4. First Printing. Month, 200X 10 9 8 7 6 5 4 3 2 1

FINDER

CARLA SPEED MCNEIL

TALISMAN

MY BOOK
anD ART:
SHALL:
NeVeR:
PART:

DEDICATION:

to the kid
with the
book;

everywhere

INTRO:
MAMA'S
LITTLE
STRANGEL

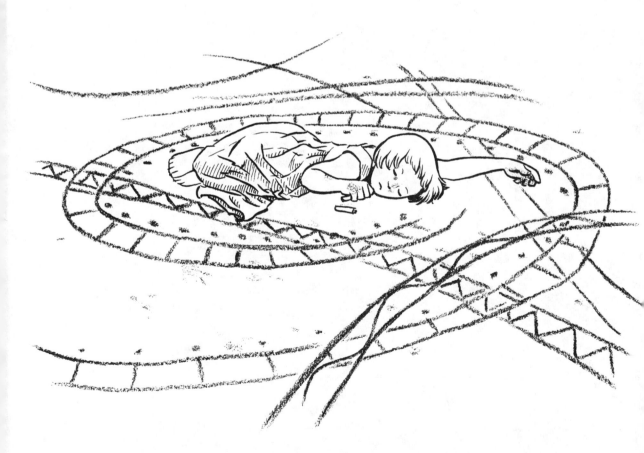

BUT I WAS JUST GONNA FIX THAT CAB'NET DOOR THAT BITES YOUR HAND...

≡SIGH≡

BABY, IT DOESN'T REALLY BITE ME. I JUST SAID THAT TO BE SILLY.

IT'S JUST A STICKY LATCH, AND THE KNOB GRABS MY-- CATCHES MY THUMB IF I GRAB IT JUST THE--

POP

CLUNK!

hsss! AOW! owowow!

OW! daah-gunnit!

mm-hm♪

CHAPTER ONE:

child of the pure unclouded brow

THE GREATEST GIFT I WAS EVER GIVEN WAS A BOOK.

IT WAS GIVEN TO ME BY A FRIEND OF THE FAMILY, WHO OFTEN TURNED UP UNEXPECTEDLY, LIKE A NEIGHBORHOOD CAT.

HIS VOICE WAS LOW AND GRAVELLY. THE ORDINARIEST THINGS IN THE WORLD SOUNDED DIFFERENT WHEN **HE** SAID THEM.

MY MOM SAID HIS VOICE WAS ROUGH BECAUSE HE WAS ALONE TOO MUCH, BUT THAT DIDN'T MAKE ANY SENSE.

I WAS SEVEN, BUT I HADN'T HAD MUCH SCHOOLING, AND I COULDN'T READ.

ALL I KNEW WAS, THOSE HEIROGLYPHS OPENED UP WHEN HE READ TO ME

CHAPTER ONE:
THE BRIDE.

AND I FELL IN.

"...WHEN SUDDENLY A WHITE RABBIT WITH PINK EYES RAN CLOSE BY HER ...."

"...HENCEFORTH SHE KNEW SHE MUST GROW UP. YOU ALWAYS KNOW AFTER YOU ARE TWO. TWO IS THE BEGINNING OF THE END ..."

"...MY OWN GARDEN IS MY OWN GARDEN,' THE GIANT SAID. 'ANYONE CAN UNDERSTAND THAT, AND I WILL ALLOW NOBODY TO PLAY IN IT BUT MYSELF.' AND HE BUILT A HIGH WALL..."

"...IT WAS FOURTEEN YEARS OF HELL, ALL TOLD, BUT SHE HARDLY KNEW IT. FOR MOST OF THOSE YEARS SHE EXISTED IN A DAZE SO DEEP IT WAS LIKE DEATH...."

"...THE LAMB SAID, 'KILL ME AND EAT ME. IF YOU DON'T CRACK ANY OF MY BONES, THE FIRST LIGHT OF THE FOLLOWING DAY WILL RESTORE ME TO LIFE ...'"

"'...I CAN'T ANSWER THAT,' REPLIED THE WEREWOLF. 'LIKE ALL GOOD DOGS, I'M A CYNIC, AND THEREFORE A LITTLE BLIND. I CAN ONLY SEE THINGS AS THEY ARE, NOT AS THEY OUGHT TO BE ...'"

IT FADED AWAY. I COULDN'T REMEMBER IT. LIKE A DREAM.

JUST BITS AND PIECES.

BUT IT WAS SO *VIVID.*

I COULDN'T BELIEVE ALL THAT CAME OUT OF THOSE RIDICULOUS INK SQUIGGLES.

STRANGEST OF ALL...

...IT ALL SEEMED SOMEHOW TO BE ABOUT **ME**... MY HOME.

I KNEW OUR FRIEND WOULDN'T BE AROUND FOR VERY LONG.

THERE WAS NEVER ANY TELLING WHEN HE'D SHOW UP OR HOW LONG HE'D STAY;

JUST THAT IT WOULDN'T BE LONG, EVER.

YOU DOG!

MY FAMILY GRUMBLED ABOUT HOW UNRELIABLE HE WAS.

HE'D COME AND THEN HE'D GO. WHAT'S SO HARD TO PREDICT ABOUT **THAT**?

SO I HAD HIM READ ME MORE OF IT EVERY CHANCE I GOT. OH, I *PREYED* ON THAT MAN.

AND THE BOOK WAS *HUGE.* OTHER STORY-BOOKS WERE OVER SO **SOON**...FAR, **FAR** TOO SOON, **ALWAYS.**

HE *NEVER* CAME TO THE END. IT WAS HEAVEN.

THE BOOK WAS FULL OF MISTS AND MONSTERS.

OHH, I'M SO GLAD YOU CAME BACK...

THE PEOPLE IN IT WERE SURROUNDED BY HUGE THINGS THEY DIDN'T QUITE UNDERSTAND.

JUST THE MAN I NEED.

≡SIGH≡ CAN YOU KILL MY HUSBAND FOR ME?

..WHAT??

SIGH

YOUUUU... WHORE!

TELL 'EM T' GO AWAAAY.... PIG-FUCKA... I DON' WANNANY VISITORS... OH SHIT IT BURNS!

EHHHHH... SOB HELP HELP AAAAAAA

BRIGHAM. HE, UH...

FUCK! YOU FUCKIN' BITCH!

...HASN'T BEEN ALL THAT COHERENT SINCE WE BROUGHT HIM HOME FROM THE HOSPITAL.

≡WHINE≡

IT'S... HARDER ON US THAN I THOUGHT IT WOULD BE.

13

I LOVED MY MOTHER. SHE WAS LIKE THE QUEEN OF THE FOREST IN THE STORY.

IN MY BOOK IT SAID THAT HER NAME, "EMMA," MEANT "GRANDMOTHER" OR "ANCESTRESS." I DIDN'T SEE HOW SUCH A SHORT NAME COULD MEAN TWO DIFFERENT THINGS, BUT I WAS EAGER TO FIND OUT.

YOU WANT TO LEARN TO **READ,** MY DARLIN'?

I THINK THAT'S A **FINE** AMBITION.

IT'S A RATHER ARCHAIC SKILL, LIKE PENMANSHIP, BUT I DO THINK THE OLD WAYS HAVE A LOT OF CHARM.

YOUR GRANDMOTHER WILL BE THRILLED...

CAN'T YOU READ, MAMA?

ME? OH, OF COURSE-- I WENT TO A TRADITIONAL SCHOOL. BUT I NEVER LIKED READING FOR PLEASURE; IT'S BAD FOR THE EYES.

LOTS OF PEOPLE WHO **CAN** READ **DON'T;** WHAT WITH SKULL COMPUTERS AND ACCESS-JACKS, EVEN PROFESSORS AT THE COLLEGE MISS IT LESS AND LESS.

MY SWEET OLD-FASHIONED GIRL. GIVE ME A KISS, LOVE. I HAVE TO GO TO WORK NOW.

MY MOTHER MADE HER LIVING OFF OF GETTING LOST IN HER OWN WORLD.

I GUESS WE'RE VERY MUCH ALIKE.

USUALLY WHEN PEOPLE FIND OUT THEY'RE LIKE ONE ANOTHER, IT'S SUPPOSED TO BRING THEM CLOSER TOGETHER.

THAT'S HOW IT IS IN BOOKS.

16

HE DIDN'T SEEM TO **TRY** TO DO A DIFFERENT VOICE FOR EACH CHARACTER.

BUT I HEARD THEM ANYWAY.

...THE **TERRIBLE** THING ABOUT THE PREACHER MAN WAS HOW HIS VOICE COULD BE SO SWEET AND SOFT, WHEN HIS HEART WAS AS DRY AS A WASPS' NEST, AND JUST AS HOT WITH KILLIN'.

"CHILDREN?" HE CALLED. "CHILLLL-DREN?"

"I CAN FEEL MYSELF GETTIN' AW-FUL **MAD**..."

"YOU COME ON OUT WHEN I COUNT THREE, NOW.

"ONE...

"TWO...

AAA! AAA! AAA!!

DON'T PUT THOSE THINGS ON ME! AAA! AAA!

GASP GASP GASPP

OH **OH** FUCKERS, FUCKERS 'RE CLOSING **IN**.... **KEEP** THAT L'TTLE SHIT **AWAY** FROM ME... **AAH**... YOUUU....

YOU'VE BEEN A **DISAPPOINTMENT** TO ME SINCE THE DAY Y'R MUTHER **FARTED** YOU OUT OF 'ER **WOMB**

uh!

OHHH, MAN.... UH UH AAA!!

OOH... SNIVEL WHINE WHINE

SHIT LICKER! BETTER RUN YOU you

LINE UP, YOU LIMP-DICK MONKEY FUCKS!

SONSA BITCHES THINK SMARTER THAN T ARMY IN OE ODD A

I KNEW I DONT GIV A SHIT WHO AR E R

THAT ALL STORIES LIKE THIS

YOU THINK YOU K WHAT PA IS? WEL I'M G SHOW Y WHO SUFF

YOU PIECE 'A SHIT! YOU LOUSY PIECE 'A SHIT!

ALWAYS COME DOWN TO SOMEBODY

HAVING TO OVERCOME SOME AWFUL FEAR.

THAT'S FINE FOR FICTION.

WHEN HE LEFT

(SUDDENLY, AS ALWAYS)

HE LEFT WITHOUT FINISHING IT.

I WAS DYING.

I'M DYING.

NOTHING TO DO BUT SETTLE FOR LESS.

I STARTED WITH MY BIG SISTER.

HM?

RACHEL?

WILL YOU READ MY BOOK TO ME?

YOUR BOOK? WHY?

...OH, I GET IT. THIS OLD THING HAS NO VOICE-CHIP AT ALL.

≡SIGH≡ SURE, HONEY.

OKAY THEN...

"CHAPTER NINETEEN: THE FOREST GLEN."

"THERE WAS NOTHING TO DO FOR IT UNTIL THEY WERE QUITE DRIED OFF. SO MARCIE AND HER FRIEND--

HEY, ISN'T THAT COOL! YOUR NAME'S IN THIS!

I ALWAYS LOVE TO SEE MY NAME IN A STORY EVEN IF IT IS JUST A COINCIDENCE.

"SO MARCIE AND HER FRIEND MADE THEMSELVES COMFORTABLE ON A LOG IN A PATCH OF SUNLIGHT, AND WERE QUITE COMFORTABLE.
"PRESENTLY WOLFE YAWNED AND STRETCHED AND OPENED HIS PACK--"
"--FINALLY PRODUCING A PAPER BAG OF SMALL RASPBERRIES, A HALF-LOAF OF BREAD, AND A LARGE SOFT CHEESE, WRAPPED IN A CLOTH COVERED WITH BLUISH-GREEN OR GREENISH-BLUE SPOTS."
"THIS WAS A GREAT RELIEF TO MARCIE, WHO, UNTIL WOLFE HAD PULLED OUT THE FOOD, HADN'T REALIZED HOW HUNGRY SHE WAS.
THEY SET AFTER THEIR LUNCHEON WITH A WILL, AND SOON FINISHED IT OFF."
"AFTER THEY HAD FINISHED, THE SUN'S LIGHT WAS SLANTING DOWN RATHER MORE STEEPLY THAN BEFORE, AND MARCIE SUGGESTED THAT THEY HAD BEST BE MOVING ON.
'WOLFIE,' SAID SHE, 'THE DAY'S GETTING AWAY FROM US, AND WE STILL HAVE A LONG WAY TO GO. HADN'T WE BEST BE MOVING ON?'"
"YES, I SUPPOSE SO," REPLIED THE OTHER, 'ELSE WE'LL LOSE THE LIGHT ALTOGETHER, AND BE OBLIGED TO STAY HERE FOR THE NIGHT.'
'OH NO,' SAID MARCIE. 'WE MUSTN'T DO THAT. LET'S BE ON OUR IMMEDIATE
THAT'S NOT IT!
WHAT--?
YOU'RE READING IT WRONG!

SO.
I'D TRIED **ONE** SISTER. NOT MUCH POINT IN TRYING THE OTHER ONE.

NOT THAT LYNNE WAS MY *SISTER,* EXACTLY. SHE WAS REALLY A BOY WHO'D BEEN RAISED AS A GIRL AND WAS NOW SORT OF BOTH.

NO, I DIDN'T GET IT EITHER. AT THAT AGE YOU GO ALONG WITH A LOT.

BUT BOY-OH-BOY COULD SHE BE A SON OF A *BITCH.*

SIGH

KID, YOU CAN STOP MOPING SO LOUD ANY TIME.

SIGH.

DON'T HASSLE ME WITH YOUR **SIGHS,** MARCIE.

BUT SIR...

AND DON'T CALL ME "SIR".

SO?

RACHEL TOOK MY BOOK AWAY.

IT'S MINE. IT WAS MY BIRTHDAY PRESENT.

SO?

IT'S NOT FAIR!

SO?

LOOK, MARS. THIS IS NOT *SOCCER.* THIS IS DEALING WITH PEOPLE WHO HAVE **POWER** OVER YOU; IN THIS CASE, OUR SISTER.

THERE **ARE** NO RULES AND THERE **IS** NO "FAIR".

BUT...

IF YOU WANT YOUR BOOK, GO **GET** IT.

I'LL GET A WHIPPIN'.

FROM RACHEL?

≡SNORT≡

SOUNDS LIKE YOU HAVE ONE OF *THOSE* DECISIONS TO MAKE.

IS THE PRICE YOU MIGHT PAY WORTH WHAT YOU MIGHT GET?

BUT I CAN'T EVEN *READ* IT.

WOULD YOU READ ME MY BOOK?

NO.

SIGH.

I DON'T **CARE** WHAT COLORS I LOOK BEST IN! I DON'T **WANT** A CUBBY-HOLE WITH MY NAME ON IT! I WANT TO **LEARN** TO **READ!**

MMM. WOW.

A SCHOOL OUR MOTHER PICKED OUT TURNS OUT TO BE FULL OF FLAKES.

A-**MAY**-ZING.

WELL, WHAT DID YOU THINK?

Y'THINK THEY WERE GONNA TEACH YOU TO READ ALL IN ONE DAY?

CLICK.

W... W-WELL... YEAH!

IF YOU **REALLY** WANNA LEARN TO READ *FAST*, I CAN FIX *THAT.*

EE EEE!! NO HOOK UP!

THAT—IS—CORRECT.

HOLY SHIT!

LIKE MAGIC, ALL OF A SUDDEN ONE DAY I COULD READ MY OWN NAME!

M! A! R! C! I! E! MARCIE! THAT—IS—CORRECT.

MY NAME WAS ALL I COULD READ, BUT HEY! MY NAME WAS IN MY BOOK! I COULD READ MY NAME IN MY BOOK! ON EVERY PAGE!

GONE

?

GONE GONE GONE

!

GONE

GONE

MAMA... WHERE'S MY BOOK?

OH, THAT. I GAVE IT TO THE RECYCLER LAST WEEK, DARLIN'.

OH, HONEY. THOSE OLD-FASHIONED PAPER-PULP BOOKS ARE *PERISHABLE.* IT WOULD ONLY HAVE GONE TO ROT; IT WAS ALREADY TURNING YELLOW.

OH, BABY, DON'T CRY...

MARCIE, THERE'S NOTHING TO CRY OVER... I SCANNED IT INTO THE HOUSE LIBRARY. IT ISN'T LOST AT ALL. ANY TIME YOU WANT TO, YOU CAN USE YOUR HOOKUP, AND IT'LL BE JUST LIKE HAVING THE REAL THING. YOU CAN TOUCH IT, HOLD IT, WHATEVER; IT ISN'T GONE AT ALL.

"I HAD *NO IDEA* IT WAS SO IMPORTANT TO HER. IT WAS A GIFT FROM *JAEGER?*

"OH DEAR. HE WILL TEASE ME..."

"MOM, EVEN IF SHE *IS* ONLY SEVEN, IT *WAS* **HERS.** YOU HAD NO RIGHT TO THROW IT OUT.

"I DO THINK SHE'S OVER-REACTING..."

"WELL, KID, WHAT DO YOU WANT ME TO SAY?

"IF YOU'D PUT IT SOMEPLACE **SAFE,** THEY COULDN'T'VE DONE THIS TO YOU..."

THE GREATEST GIFT I EVER HAD TAKEN AWAY FROM ME WAS A BOOK.

CHAPTER 2:

melan-choly maiden

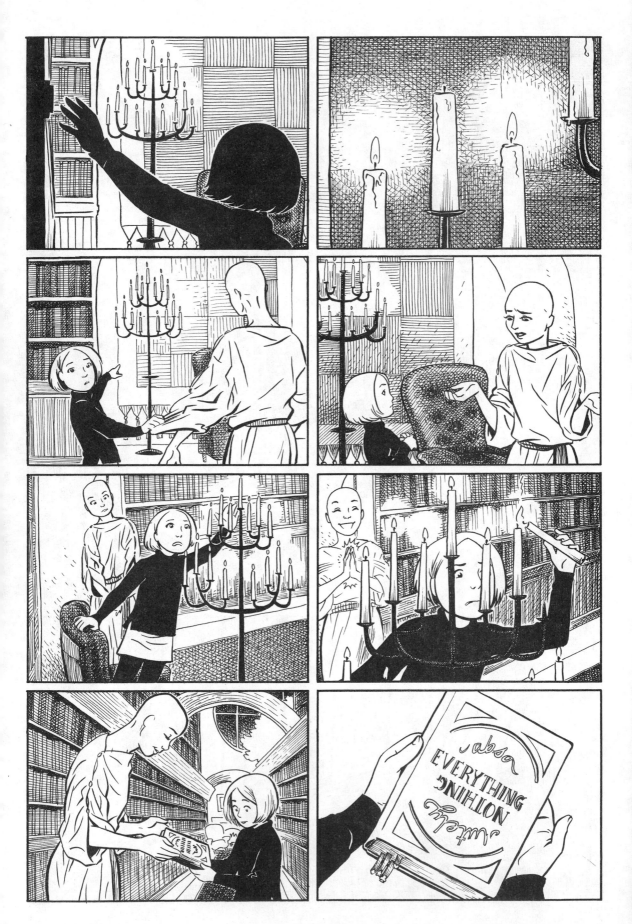

UFF!

SIGH.

WHEN I WAS SEVEN, I LOST A BOOK.

WELL, ACTUALLY, MY MOTHER THREW IT OUT.

BUT I'VE LEARNED NOT TO THINK OF IT THAT WAY.

EVER SINCE THEN, I'VE HAD THIS RECURRING DREAM.

I'M TOLD IT'S A VERY **TRITE** DREAM. THAT EVERYBODY HAS THIS DREAM FROM TIME TO TIME.

SOMETIMES I CAN **FEEL** THAT BOOK'S BINDING IN MY HANDS BEFORE I LOSE IT.

IT'S A SAD THING WHEN EVEN YOUR DREAMS ARE CLICHES.

I DON'T KNOW WHEN MY BROTHER BECAME THE BEDROCK OF MY LIFE.

WE HAD A MOTHER AND AN OLDER SISTER, BUT HE MADE THE RULES.

ONE OF THE HARD, FAST RULES WAS I DIDN'T DARE CRY IN FRONT OF HIM.

IT'S NOT THAT HE WAS UNSYMPATHETIC. HE'D HUG ME, AND DOLE OUT MINTS, AND WAIT FOR ME TO CALM DOWN.

BUT THEN HE'D EXACT SOME INCREDIBLY BRUTAL REVENGE AGAINST WHOEVER OR WHATEVER HAD UPSET ME.

SOMEHOW MY TEARS ENFURIATED HIM.

AND THERE WAS NO SLAP ON THE WRIST IN LYNNE'S BOOK OF RETRIBUTION. IT WAS THE JUGULAR OR NOTHING.

SO I DIDN'T DARE CRY OVER THE BOOK I LOST.

MARVELLO THE MYSTIC SEES A B-MINUS IN YOUR FUTURE.

C IF SHE TAKES OFF FOR BREVITY.

SO I HAD TO LEARN TO HOLD IN.

I HATE TO CRY, ANYWAY.

IN THE EARLY DAYS OF LEARNING TO HOLD IN, I USED TO APOLOGIZE FOR CRYING.

≋AH--HUH-HUHH≋ IT'LL STOP ≋SKNKK≋ IT'LL STOP-- I'LL BE ≋HUHH≋ I'LL BE OKAY IN A MINUTE---

LIKE IT WAS A CUT FINGER THAT WOULD STOP BLEEDING, OR HICCUPS.

I HAD THIS ONGOING DAYDREAM WHICH MADE IT A LOT EASIER. IT INSULATED ME FROM WORRY AND BOREDOM.

WHEN I WASN'T READING, I WAS EMBROIDERING MY DAYDREAM WITH DETAILS FROM MY BOOKS.

ANY BOOK WAS FAIR GAME....

NOT AS HIGH

THE HILLS ARE

THE SEA SO DEEP

AS A DREAM

"YOU ARE A LITTLE POT FULL OF SONGS, AND WHEN YOU CRY, THE POT BREAKS AND ALL THE SONGS SPILL OUT UGLY."

"...I ASK FOR SO LITTLE. JUST LET ME RULE YOU, AND YOU CAN HAVE EVERYTHING THAT YOU WANT. JUST FEAR ME; LOVE ME, DO AS I SAY, AND I WILL BE YOUR SLAVE!"

AFTER WILLIAMS

"LOOK, EVERYONE," SAID THE STAR. "I'M BURNING SO BRIGHT!" AND THEN IT WENT NOVA. AND WHEN THE LIGHT FADED, THE STAR WAS NOWHERE TO BE SEEN.
THE MORAL OF THIS STORY IS OBVIOUS."

"...HE STARED IN FASCINATION AT THE HOURGLASS, AT THE PHOSPHORESCENT CRYSTALS IN THE THICK GLOBE WHICH GAVE EACH INFANT HIS BIRTHRIGHT-- THE RADIOACTIVE TIMEFLOWER. HE STARED AT HIS OWN HAND, BLINKING RED-BLACK, RED-BLACK..."

"THERE WERE PLENTY OF RINGS IN THE AIR BUT ALL OF THEM WERE PALE IN COLOR WHICH WARNED ME OFF. LIGHT YELLOWS USUALLY EXITED IN PLACES SUCH AS EIGHTY KILOMETERS DUE SOUTH OF THE MOON, TEN METERS FROM THE BOTTOM OF MINDANAO DEEP, THE TOP OF ANNAPURNA, AND THE LIKE. BESIDES, I WASN'T READY TO GO BACK..."

"SOMEHOW, IT WAS HOTTER THEN: A BLACK DOG SUFFERED ON A SUMMER'S DAY; BONY MULES HITCHED TO HOOVER CARTS FLICKED FLIES IN THE SWELTERING SHADE OF THE LIVE OAKS IN THE SQUARE. MEN'S STIFF COLLARS WILTED BY NINE IN THE MORNING. LADIES BATHED BEFORE NOON, AFTER THEIR THREE-O'CLOCK NAPS, AND BY NIGHTFALL WERE LIKE SOFT TEA-CAKES WITH FROSTINGS OF SWEAT AND SWEET TALCUM..."

I CANNOT NAME

MY HEART HAS SOUGHT

A THING

LYNNE DISAPPROVED OF CONSUMPTION WITHOUT PRODUCTION.

IF ALL YOU DO IS READ, WATCH, LISTEN, AND NEVER *THINK*, NEVER *ACT*, YOU ARE EATING WITHOUT BUILDING BONE OR MUSCLE.

FRANKLY, YOU ARE EATING WITHOUT EVEN *SHITTING*.

WORK *EVERY* DAY, KID, EVEN IF YOU *DO* THINK IT'S JUST SHIT. MENTAL CONSTIPATION IS THE WORLD'S WORST SLOW POISON. SO *CHOP-CHOP!* ON TO THE NEXT.

LYNNE ENCOURAGED ME TO WRITE IT ALL DOWN.

AT FIRST, I WAS WORRIED THAT MY DAYDREAMS WERE TOO PERSONAL, THAT IT WOULD BE INCREDIBLY EMBARRASSING TO LET ANYBODY READ THEM.

HA!

I *LIKED* THE KIDS IN MY HALF-TOON AT MY NEW SCHOOL. I WAS WILLING TO TAKE THE RISK OF MORTAL EMBARRASSMENT BY BARING MY SOUL TO THEM.

THEY'RE OKAY KIDS, THEY REALLY ARE... THEY *TRIED* TO BE COOL ABOUT IT WHEN THEY HAD TO TELL ME MY STORIES WERE *BORING!*

BORING?

HOW COULD SOMETHING *I* FOUND SO ABSORBING BE *BORING?* HOW COULD WHAT I FELT SO STRONGLY LEAVE *THEM* SO UNMOVED?

WHY DIDN'T THEY FEEL WHAT I FELT?

LYNNE SAID IT WAS A MATTER OF TECHNIQUE.

I WAS GRIMLY DETERMINED TO LEARN.

LYNNE ALWAYS HAD MONEY. IF I WANTED A BOOK, I GOT IT.

I KNEW MY HOME CITY AS A HUGE EMPTY SPACE WITH CONSTELLATIONS OF BOOKSTORES AND LIBRARIES. I BOUGHT, BORROWED, DEVOURED.

"...RIVETING!" "...ENGROSSING!" "...GOOD!"

NOT FOR YEARS DID I REALIZE THAT I WAS HOPING THAT THE TALENT IN MY FAVORITE BOOKS WOULD RUB OFF ON ME.

I HOPED TO LEARN WRITING BY OSMOSIS, I GUESS.

I DID REALIZE THAT HOW-TO BOOKS MADE ME FEEL STALE. THEY LOOK SO PROMISING ON THE SHELF; THEY MAKE WRITING LOOK SO EASY.

BUT WHEN YOU GET 'EM HOME, THEY'VE TURNED INTO JUST ANOTHER DRY LIST OF BORING RULES.

EVEN SO, I STILL COULDN'T STOP BUYING THEM.

BAHGIN!

ONE DAY I'D SCRIBBLE LIKE MAD, TYPE AWAY LIKE A PERKING COFFEE POT. WHO NEEDS THE MUSE? IT WAS ALL CRAP, BUT WHO CARED? NOT ME?

THE NEXT DAY I'D SWEAR I WOULDN'T PUT DOWN A WORD UNTIL IT WAS PERFECT IN MY MIND (WHICH MEANT, OF COURSE, THAT I NEVER PUT DOWN A WORD, PERIOD).

THEN I'D TRY TO GO BACK TO THE THINGS THAT EXCITE ME; THE FOUNDATIONS OF MY DAY-DREAM.

THAT USUALLY LEADS ME BACK TO MY LOST BOOK.

THERE WAS A COPY OF MY BOOK IN THE HOUSE'S COMPUTER. I COULD CALL IT UP ANYTIME I LIKED.

WITH MY STUDENT-LEVEL ACCESS JACK, I COULD SEE THE BOOK AS IF IT WAS REAL. I COULD HOLD IT IN MY HAND AND EVEN *OPEN* IT.

I JUST COULDN'T READ IT.

SOMEHOW, THE FILE HAD BEEN CORRUPTED.

EACH MONTH, THE HOUSE DUTIFULLY MADE A PERFECT COPY OF THE BAD FILE.

BUT I'M NOT UPSET ABOUT IT. I'VE LEARNED TO FACE THE WORLD WITH A COMFORTABLY AMBIVALENT INERTIA. I SHOULD CARE, BUT I CONSIDER MYSELF LUCKY THAT I DON'T.

LYNNE TELLS ME THAT THAT'S WHY MY WRITING IS SO DULL.

YOU KNOW, MARCE, MOVIE-MAKERS TALK ABOUT THIS ALL THE TIME. HOW IT'S THEIR JOB TO MAKE THE AUDIENCE FEEL WHAT THEY'RE SUPPOSED TO.

I HATE MOVIES.

≡TSK≡ WE **KNOW** YOU HATE MOVIES. BUT FACE IT-- NO BOOK CAN MAKE ANYBODY FEEL WHAT'S GOING ON AS INTENSELY AS IF IT'S REALLY HAPPENING.

OH. THAT'S NOT TRUE--

LOOK-- YOU KNOW *I* LIKE TO READ TOO, BUT IT'S JUST *NOT* THE SAME THING.

OH, COME WITH US. HOW CAN YOU GET TO BE A WRITER IF YOU DON'T EVER DO ANYTHING?

I HARDLY THINK THAT GOING TO THE MOVIES REALLY COUNTS AS A BIG, DRAMATIC, OUT-ON-A-LIMB, LIFE-ALTERING ADVENTURE....

FOR SOMEBODY WHO GOES AS RARELY AS YOU DO, IT DOES.

YOU'LL LIKE THIS ONE-- THAT FOOTAGE YOUR BROTHER SOLD TO STUDIOSIMA IS IN IT.

UNBELIEVABLE, HOW MANY PEOPLE *LIVE* FOR GOING TO THE MOVIES.

FOR PEOPLE WITHOUT THE JACK, A MOVIE IS JUST PICTURES AND SOUND.

JUST NOISE AND FLICKER, GUARANTEED TO GIVE ME AN INSTANT HEADACHE.

TONS OF PEOPLE WHO *DON'T* HAVE JACKS STILL LOVE THE MOVIES, WHICH I *REALLY* DON'T UNDERSTAND.

I MEAN, WITHOUT THE JACK ENGAGED, YOU CAN'T EVEN *SEE* THE SCREEN, OR EVEN *HEAR* OVER PEOPLE WHISPERING.

WITH THE JACK, IT'S LIKE THERE'S ONLY THE SCREEN AND YOU.

SO.

LOT OF FOLKS MAKE A LIVING SELLING RECORDINGS TO MOVIE STUDIOS. NOT JUST SCENES, STILLS, AND MUSIC -- SOME PEOPLE SELL RECORDINGS OF NERVOUS IMPULSES. ANYTHING VIVID IS FAIR GAME.

SO YOU LAUGH AT JOKES THAT AREN'T FUNNY

--SOMETIMES THEY RUN HUMOR AND FEAR RIGHT ON TOP OF EACH OTHER, PRESUMABLY TO SUGARCOAT THE FEAR, BUT I DUNNO--

AND FALL IN LOVE WITH WEIRD-LOOKING ACTORS--

--MOST MOVIES JUST HAVE A MOOD-TRACK, LIKE A SOUNDTRACK, THAT'S WHAT MOST DIRECTORS PREFER, ACCORDING TO LYNNE--

BUT FANCY THEATERS DON'T USE MOOD-TRACKS THEY HIRE CONDUCTORS

--NOBODY CAN TELL A JOKE THEY HEARD IN A MOVIE "YOU JUST HAVE TO SEE IT" AND THAT'S JUST HOW THE STUDIOS WANT IT TO BE--

IT'S A VERY INTENSE EXPERIENCE.

I JUST DON'T UNDERSTAND HOW PEOPLE *ENJOY* GETTING YANKED AROUND LIKE THAT.

OPEN TEAR-DUCTS, APPLY PLIERS...

I FEEL LIKE SOMEBODY PICKED ME UP BY MY HEAD AND SHOOK ME LIKE A MARACA.

I KNOW WHAT I *DO* WANT. I WANT THE BOOK I LOST. THE ONE MY MOM'S BOYFRIEND USED TO READ TO ME.

IN A REGULAR STORY, RIGHT ABOUT NOW, I'D *FIND* THAT BOOK. LIKE *MAGIC*. I'D JUST TURN MY HEAD AND THERE IT WOULD BE.

AND I WOULDN'T BELIEVE IT, NO MATTER HOW MUCH I'D WANT TO.

IN *JAEGER'S* STORY, THE MAGIC ALWAYS HAD STRANGE RULES.

IN *THAT* STORY, I'D GET WHAT I WANT, BUT I'D STILL HAVE TO

--TO--

45

There couldn't be another one like it. It was hand-bound especially for me. It was unique.

I'd been in this shop before, but not for a long time-- these little places do appear and disappear suddenly--

It must have been sold and sold again, circling around the city for years until it came back to me--

Just like Jaeger

Who gave it to me.

GOING OUT OF BUSINESS
CLOSED

LICENSE DISPUTE

CORIANDER

COME AND BUY IT OR WE'LL THROW IT TO THE HOGS!

DO NOT CROSS · DO NOT CROSS · DO NOT CROSS

This place never had many books of interest to me, but it smelled of the proprietor's sweet pipe smoke--

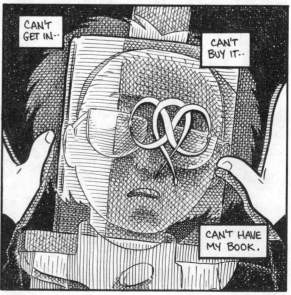

Can't get in--

Can't buy it--

Can't have my book.

NO.

NO.

TIME TO BE A GROWN-UP.

I FOUND IT, BUT I CAN'T HAVE IT.

AND I AM *NOT* GOING TO SIT ON THE CURB AND HOPE SOMEBODY'LL BUY THIS PLACE AND OPEN IT UP AGAIN. THAT'S PATHETIC AND BESIDES IT *ISN'T* GONNA HAPPEN.

SIGH.

IT ISN'T WORTH HOPING FOR.

EVEN IF THIS SHOP *DOES* REOPEN, YOU CAN *BET* THAT THIS PARTICULAR BOOK WON'T STILL BE ON THE SHELF.

FIRST THING A NEW OWNER DOES IS CLEAR OUT MOST OF THE OLD STOCK.

AND THAT'S WHAT IT IS, REALLY. OLD STOCK.

MAYBE THE RECYCLERS *WILL* GET IT THIS TIME.

OR A LIBRARY.

OR MAYBE IT'LL JUST GO INTO THE OLD PIPE-SMOKING GUY'S ATTIC, ALONG WITH ALL THE OTHER UNSOLD BOOKS. MAYBE... SOMEDAY... IT'LL COME BACK TO ME AGAIN.

I'LL GO MY WAY, AND THE BOOK WILL GO ITS WAY. THIS IS JUST A CHANCE MEETING BETWEEN OLD FRIENDS.

A CASUAL, BITTERSWEET HELLO--

--TO SOMEBODY WHO CAN'T STOP TO TALK--

--SOME STRAY WITH NO HOME--

SOMEONE WHO CAN NEVER BE YOURS--

49

NNNNNG!

WHAT'S THE MATTER, MARCIE?

NOTHING.

WHAT'S THE MATTER, MARCIE?

NOTHING, SIR.

?

PPP HAA HA HA HA HA HA HA HA HA HA!!

HO-HO-O, **MAN!**

THIS IS IT, ISN'T IT? THIS IS THE ONE HE GAVE YOU WHEN YOU WERE SEVEN.

YES SIR.

I THOUGHT SO. YOU BAWLED OVER THIS THING FOR WEEKS.

SAD, SAD.

UP TO HIS OLD TRICKS, I SEE.

WHAT DO YOU MEAN?

THIS IS ONE OF THOSE GIMMICK BOOKS. YOU'D FILL OUT YOUR KID'S NAME, AGE, FRIENDS' NAMES, FAVORITE FOODS, PETS' NAMES... THE COMPANY SENDS *YOU* A STORYBOOK WITH ALL THAT INFORMATION INSERTED.

IT WAS JUST A SCAM, A WAY TO START DOSSIERS ON FUTURE CONSUMERS AT A REALLY YOUNG AGE. ODD.

ALL THAT WAS OUTLAWED YEARS AGO. THIS THING'S A RELIC.

HE MUST'VE PICKED IT UP BECAUSE IT HAS YOUR NAME IN IT.

MARCELLA, Y'KNOW... IT'S A POPULAR NAME IN MEDAWAR CLAN.

≡TSK≡ I.Q. 88 CHILDREN'S FICTION. ALL THE CHARACTERS DO IS *TALK* AND *EAT*.

WELL, THAT'S JAEGER ALL OVER. A BEAUTIFUL COVER ON A PIECE OF SHIT.

MAY I HAVE MY BOOK, PLEASE?

DON'T TAKE IT TOO HARD. HE DOES SERVE UP SPELLBINDING BULLSHIT.

HE USED TO DO IT TO US TOO, Y'KNOW.

WHAT DID HE DO?

HE'D MAKE THINGS UP, TELL STORIES, WHEN HE WAS SUPPOSED TO BE READING TO US.

HE'D JUST BULLSHIT, AND TURN THE PAGES WHENEVER HE FELT LIKE IT.

RACHEL ALWAYS LET HIM GET AWAY WITH IT.

RACHEL →

← JAEGER

I MADE HIM STICK TO THE STORY EVEN IF IT WAS A STINKBOMB.

WHY?

WELL...

I GUESS BECAUSE I WANTED TO READ. I LEARNED TO READ BY FOLLOWING THE WORDS WHILE SOMEONE ELSE READ TO ME.

≡ UNH ≡

I REALLY WANT THIS STORY... BUT IT DOESN'T EXIST!

IF I WANT TO READ IT, I HAVE TO WRITE IT, AND I CAN'T!

I'M NOT GOOD ENOUGH TO GET EVEN HALF OF IT RIGHT!

≡ AHEM ≡

KID...

IF A THING IS WORTH DOING, IT'S WORTH DOING BADLY.

CHAPTER 3:

dreaming eyes of wonder

58

NOT MUCH TO SAY ABOUT ME BESIDES THE FACT THAT I SPEND MOST OF MY TIME CHASING BOOKS AND I USED TO BELIEVE IN MAGIC.

NOT *FLASHY* MAGIC. NOT LIGHT-SHOWS AND SMOKE-FIGURES AND PARTING THE SEA.

STUFF LIKE...THINGS THAT HAPPEN RIGHT IN THE CORNER OF YOUR EYE. DOORS-- ORDINARY DOORS THAT MIGHT UNEXPECTEDLY OPEN ON SOME ALIEN SCENE. FLICKERING LIGHT THAT CAN MAKE A STATUE BLINK AND BREATHE.

LIKE... CHECKING OUT AN ANTIQUE LIBRARY BOOK, AND FINDING YOUR *FATHER'S* NAME WRITTEN IN IT, IN A CHILDISH BUT UNMISTAKABLE HAND.

DIAMOND RINGS IN DEAD FISH... LOST KEYS IN BIRDS' NESTS .... VOICES IN DRAINS, EYES IN STRANGE WINDOWS.

EARL!

THE STRANGENESS OF THE WORLD, THE MERE POSSIBILITIES, THEY WERE SO EXCITING TO ME. I DIDN'T CARE, WHEN I WAS A KID, THAT PEOPLE THOUGHT I WAS COMPLETELY GOOFY.

EARL, Y'IDIOT! YOU CAN'T TAKE THAT THING THROUGH A REVOLVING DOOR!

IS IT *CONVINCING*. THAT'S THE THING... IF ONLY I COULD FIND THE RIGHT WORDS TO EXPLAIN HOW THE WEIRDNESS OF THE WORLD *IS*, THEN IT REALLY WOULD *BE* THAT WAY...

I LIKED THE IDEA OF FAIRIES AND GHOSTS AND MAGIC SWORDS AND CARDS TELLING THE FUTURE... BUT THOSE WERE FOR BOOKS. *WHY* WEREN'T THEY REAL? THEY SEEMED REAL ENOUGH WHILE I WAS READING.

ALL THESE THINGS YOU'RE CALLING MAGIC ARE *COINCIDENTAL* AT BEST.

MY BROTHER LYNNE.

BUT MAYBE THAT'S WHAT MAGIC *IS*. **SOME** THINGS THAT HAPPEN TOGETHER DON'T COUNT, BUT OTHERS **DO**; THEY FIT INTO A BIGGER PATTERN.

SOMETIMES, YES. BUT YOU SHOULD BEWARE OF SEEING THINGS THAT AREN'T THERE JUST BECAUSE YOU WANT THEM TO BE.

FALLING IN LOVE WITH AN IDEA IS DANGEROUS.

FOR A *SCIENTIST*. NOT FOR A *WRITER*.

HM. POSSIBLY.

BUT SKEPTICISM IS ALWAYS HEALTHY, PARTICULARLY IN A SELLER-DRIVEN SOCIETY LIKE OURS. EVERY SHMUCK SELLING USED RUBBER BANDS HAS A STAKE IN YOUR BEING A CREDULOUS DOOF, EASY TO PART MONEY FROM.

THERE'S A SAYING I WISH I COULD USE. "SKEPTICISM IS THE *VIRGINITY* OF THE INTELLECT. WE SHOULD CHOOSE CAREFULLY WHEN AND HOW WE GIVE IT AWAY."

-- BUT I'M NOT CONVINCED THAT VIRGINITY IS *SUCH* A VALUABLE C--

UHHHHHH GODDAM GODDAMMIT Y'WORTHLESS L GIRL!

THAT'S OUR DAD.

C'MON YA STINKIN' *COOZE!* YOUR **BODY** CAN TAKE IT BUT CAN YOUR **MIND??** FFFUG=

AND IN MY MIND, I HEAR MYSELF TELLING LYNNE "IT'S JUST A COINCIDENCE."

=SIGH=

SEEMS STRANGE THAT MY FATHER CAN STILL SCARE ME.

YOUUUUU **WHORE!**

WHUH--? GET **BACK** HERE LAZY, GOOD-FOR **COW!**

I'VE LEARNED TO DO IT ALL.

I CAN FEED HIM, MOVE HIM TO CHANGE HIS SHEETS, GIVE HIM HIS INJECTIONS.

HHAVE YOU AAA RIP YOUR OFF WIT CAN IF YOU D

I CAN PRY LOOSE HIS PAINFULLY STRONG GRIP.

BUT HE **YELLS** MOST OF THE TIME WHEN HE'S AWAKE. YELLS THE MOST **HORRIBLE** STUFF...

NO **DEMON** INFESTING A HAUNTED HOUSE EVER SAID SUCH THINGS...

HE **USED** TO QUIET DOWN FOR ME. WHEN I WAS SIX, ALL I HAD TO DO WAS TOUCH HIM OR TALK TO HIM AND HE'D STOP BUSTING OUR EARDRUMS JUST LIKE **THAT.** WE COULD ALL RELAX AND GET SOME SLEEP.

I FELT SPECIAL. NOT EXACTLY **LOVED,** BUT SPECIAL.

SOMETIMES WHEN IT'S LATE I THINK HE'LL **NEVER** SHUT UP.

SOMETIMES I THINK HE WON'T QUIET FOR ME ANY-MORE BECAUSE I'VE GROWN AND HE DOESN'T RECOGNIZE ME ANYMORE.

SOMETIMES I THINK HE WON'T STOP SCREAMING BECAUSE I'M NOT **ME** ANYMORE.

I DUNNO. IT'S LATE.

61

I'VE *HEARD* THE SOUNDS FACE-ACTORS MAKE WHEN THEY TRY TO SCREAM. IT'S PATHETIC, REALLY. THEY *RASP.* THEY HONK LIKE *GEESE.* THEY MAKE THESE STRANGLY SQUEECHES. AND THEY TEAR UP THEIR VOICES DOING IT.

I HAVE A SCREAM THAT POURS OUT OF ME LIKE HOT METAL.

IT'S LOUD AND IT'S SATISFYING AND IT'S SKULL-PIERCING. IT SETS THE BONES TO VIBRATING. IT'S FULL OF TRICKY LITTLE WAVE-FORMS THAT BYPASS THE BRAIN AND GO DIRECTLY TO THE BASE OF THE SPINE.

SADLY... NOTHING LASTS FOREVER. PEOPLE *HAVE* GOTTEN USED TO MY SCREAM IN THE SIX MONTHS THAT I'VE BEEN RECORDING IT.

OOH! YES!

NOW, ALL THEY DO IS POP OUT IN COLD SWEAT, JERK SPASTICALLY, AND GRIN WEAKLY.

OH, MY LITTLE GRAND BABY... SHE'S GOT A *GIFT!*

UNH!

OH HOW I *WISH* I COULD DO THAT TO THEM WITH MY *WRITING.*

...AND SHE'S SUCH A *PLACID* LITTLE THING USUALLY...

65

SO, HOME I GO, SATCHEL FULL OF BOOKS, PACK FULL OF DATA PLUGS, HEAD FULL OF FANTASY LIKE A CAT FULL OF KITTENS.

BUT I FEEL SO LIGHT, AS IF, IF I TOOK A DEEP ENOUGH BREATH, HELD IT, MADE A WISH, LET OUT THE BREATH JUST RIGHT, I COULD RISE UP LIKE A HELIUM BALLOON.

AND I GET HOME AND I SIT DOWN AND I START WRITING AND THEN --

SIXTEEN OUTLINES, TWELVE GENEALOGIES, EIGHT CHARACTER SHEETS, ONE ALTERNATE TIME LINE, AND THREE MAPS LATER, IT'S ALL GONE.

I DON'T KNOW WHAT I EVER FOUND EXCITING ABOUT IT. I'VE GOT A DRY HEADACHE.

THE STORY THAT'S BEEN KEEPING ME ENTERTAINED FOR WEEKS ... IT'S JUST NOT THERE ANYMORE.

MAR▶ IT'S ALIVE IN MY HEAD AND *DEAD* ON THE PAGE.

LYN▶ SO DON'T WRITE. KEEP IT FOR YOURSELF.

M▶ NO, IT DIES IN MY HEAD *TOO*. I FORGET A HUNDRED GOOD IDEAS A WEEK AND WEAR THE SHINE OFF A HUNDRED MORE.

L▶ FOREST FOR THE TREES.

M▶ ??

L▶ TOO MUCH DETAIL. IMPLY, DON'T TELL. IS A DREAMSNAKE MORE BEAUTIFUL GLIMPSED ON THE WING, OR PICKLED IN A JAR WHERE YOU CAN GET A GOOD LOOK AT IT?

L▶ GIVE READER A QUICK GLIMPSE AND MOVE ON. THEIR MINDS DO THE REST.

M▶ *HOW?*

L▶ WRITE IT ALL DOWN AS IT COMES TO YOU. REFINE IT LATER. KEEP JOURNAL.

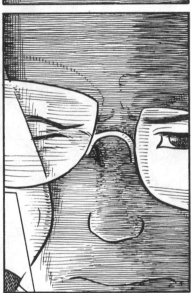

M▶ *TRIED* THAT. LIKE WRITING DOWN DREAMS. SEEMS LIKE IT'S ALL REMEMBERED PERFECTLY BUT WHEN I READ IT LATER IT'S ALL "MUGUS BLEW THE WHY HE SNARGLE = LEPT SHOE".

L▶ <G> EVERYTHING'S PROFOUND WHEN YOU'RE STONED, HUH?

L▶ GOT TO GET TO THE ROOT OF THE IDEA. WHY IT CAME TO YOU/ WHAT IT SIGNIFIES TO YOU. *PEEL IT DOWN.*

M▶ *HOW??*

L▶ *FOCUS.*

L▶ THOSE PILES OF PAPER, THAT'S CRAP. GET A BOOK TO WRITE IN. GET A BOOK WORTHY OF YOUR THOUGHTS.

L▶ *END*

I HAVE BLANK BOOKS.

THIRTEEN OF 'EM, TO BE EXACT.

EVERYBODY GIVES ME BLANK BOOKS FOR BIRTHDAYS AND HOLIDAYS.

THEY'RE ALL ANTIQUES AND GORGEOUS AND THEY'RE ALL STILL BLANK.

MOST OF 'EM, ANYWAY. THE ONES THAT AREN'T STILL BLANK--

EX LIBRIS
marcie marcie
narcie
little fareys
by and by
light the candels
of the sky

fareys

--THEY MIGHT AS WELL BE.

PIF!

AH, SHIT!

HAOOH!!

WEIRD--

THAT WAS NOT MY FATHER--

AH! GODDAMMIT!

69

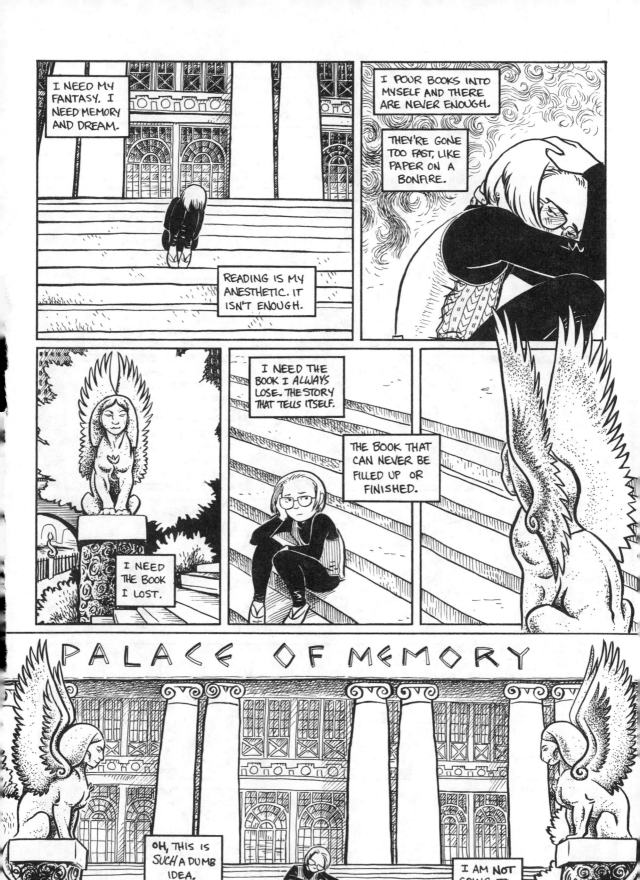

NO WAY.

I AM *NOT* GOING OFF ON SOME *FLAKY* ADVENTURE TO FIND THE *PERFECT BLANK BOOK.*

IT'S STUPID AND WEIRD AND ANYWAY IT WON'T WORK. THERE IS NO PERFECT BOOK.

MY MOTHER'S FAMILY IS FULL OF KOOKS--

THEY MAKE A LIFE OUT OF BEING WEIRD--

--THEY DO ALL SORTS OF WEIRD STUPID THINGS TO SEEM ARTSY AND INTUITIVE BUT THEY DON'T EVER PRODUCE-- **THAT'S** NOT *MAGIC*, IT'S--

--THEY MAKE UP ALL THIS RITUALISTIC BEHAVIOR BECAUSE IT *SOUNDS COOL,* NOT BECAUSE IT REALLY HELPS THEM BRING ANYTHING NEW INTO BEING.

THEY *CAWN'T* WORK WITHOUT THEIR LUCKY PINK PENCIL, OR IF THE TEMPERATURE ISN'T *JUST SO*--

--OR IF THEY'RE NOT HOME IN THEIR FAVORITE CHAIR BETWEEN THE HOURS OF TEN AND TWO--

--*OR* THEY GOTTA HAVE THEIR WRITER'S HAT OR SIX DOZEN GREEN GUMDROPS OR A DAMN TEDDY BEAR OR SOME OTHER IDIOTIC LUCKY CHARM, SOME

TALISMAN

--AND IT'S JUST AN EXCUSE NOT TO WORK, SINCE THEY *CAWN'T* WORK IF EVERYTHING'S NOT PERFECT, WHICH IT NEVER IS.

IT'S SETTING YOURSELF UP TO FAIL, THAT KIND OF MAGICAL THINKING, AND I'M *NOT* GOING TO BOTHER WITH IT.

IF IT ISN'T *ABSOLUTELY* PERFECT, I'M NOT GOING TO BOTHER WITH IT. NO MAKE-DO OR SORTA.

AND IF I DON'T FIND IT *TODAY,* THAT IS *THAT.* I CAN BLOW *ONE* DAY ON THIS FOOL'S ERRAND.

ANTIQUE BINDERY

GREYHAWK BOOKS

HOURS:

MOST SHOPS CARRY TONS OF MOVIES AND DATA-PLUGS, BUT COMPARATIVELY FEW REAL BOUND BOOKS.

EMBOSSED LEATHER

GILT EDGING

ENVIRONMENTALISTS *HATE* PAPER BOOKS. THEY SAY IT'D BE BETTER IF ALL BOOKS WERE DIGITAL FILES.

HUH..

BUT PEOPLE LIKE BOOKS...

MOSTLY FOR DECOR, MIND YOU... MY UNCLE MAG'S WHOLE LIBRARY IS BLANK. HE ORDERED FORTY YARDS OF BLUE BOOKS, AND THAT'S WHAT HE GOT.

ANY COLOR YOU WANT

DAMASK SILK

RIBBON BOOKMARKS

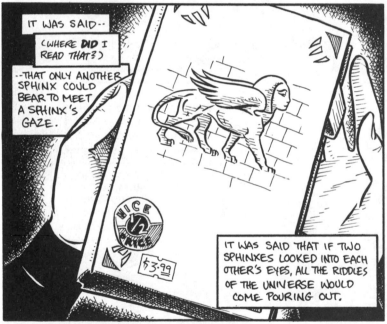

IT WAS SAID--

(WHERE *DID* I READ THAT?)

--THAT ONLY ANOTHER SPHINX COULD BEAR TO MEET A SPHINX'S GAZE.

NICE PRICE ½

$3.99

IT WAS SAID THAT IF TWO SPHINXES LOOKED INTO EACH OTHER'S EYES, ALL THE RIDDLES OF THE UNIVERSE WOULD COME POURING OUT.

MAYBE *THAT'S* WHY THE STONE GUARDIANS OF THE AMBERSON FAMILY'S PRIVATE LIBRARY (WHAT THEY CALL THE PALACE OF MEMORY)--

--MAYBE THAT'S WHY THEY FACE EACH OTHER.

THE LAST WORD IN E-BOOKS

a mere $199.99

30% DISCOUNT

VOICE CARD

SCAN·EX

FREEWARE

DECORATIVE DUST JACKETS

½ PRICE

NICE PRICE

THOSE SPHINXES ARE THE GUARDIANS OF THE GREATEST COLLECTION OF BOOKS IN THE WHOLE WORLD.

A PALACE OF BOOKS. A *TEMPLE* OF BOOKS.

THAT'S COOL.

BUT I DON'T WANT A FANCY DIGITAL DAY PLANNER. NOR DO I WANT A CHEAP CARD-BOARD JACKET TO MAKE A *PLAIN* DIGITAL DAY PLANNER LOOK FANCY.

I WANT A *BOOK*.

DATA PASS

THIS ONE--
THIS ONE--

SIMPLE BUT BEAUTIFULLY MADE. UNLINED, THICK CREAMY PAGES. HAND-STITCHED AND HAND-CUT. NO CHEESY CARTOONS, NO MESSY SMEARS OF GLUE.

BUT IT NEEDS AN ICON. A TOTEM. THE *RIGHT* SYMBOL. A SYMBOL OF ALL THE BOOKS IN THE WORLD, OF ALL MAGIC WHETHER FAKE OR REAL.

SPHINX. LIBRARY GUARDIAN. THAT GLOSSY CARDBOARD COVER, DUST JACKET FOR AN EXPENSIVE DAY PLANNER.

PERFECT.

IT WON'T MEAN A DAMN THING TO ANYONE BUT ME. BUT TO ME, IT'S THE ESSENCE. IT'S MYSTERY. THE ANCIENTS USED TO CALL THEIR RELIGIOUS RITES MYSTERIES.

IT WON'T STILL BE THERE.

'COURSE IT WILL BE. IT'S ONLY BEEN A FEW HOURS.

IF IT IS, I'LL GET IT AND CUT IT OUT, GLUE IT DOWN TO THE COVER OF *THIS* ONE. I KNOW THE KIND OF GLUE TO USE.

AND... IT'S NOT HERE.

IT'S GONE.

OF COURSE.

I HATE *WANTING* THIS. IT WON'T BE THERE. I'LL GET THAT LEAD-WEIGHT FEELING. I'LL SMOTHER.

IT *MAY* BE GONE. IT *MAY* BE *THERE*. IT *MAY* BE GONE.

GONE

ALWAYS GONE

I MAY NEVER WRITE ANYTHING IN MY BOOK. I MAY NEVER WRITE ANYTHING WORTHY OF INSCRIPTION ON THESE PAGES. BUT EVERY WORD I WRITE WILL BE WRITTEN WITH THAT ASPIRATION. IT'LL BE ENOUGH.

HERE--

75

KSSSSHT

AAAA!

AAAUWW

AA✳

HWAAAA

I DON'T REALLY BELIEVE IN REINCARNATION.

mm?

=mmblp=

BUT I HAVE STARED DOWN AT MY FATHER'S RUINED BODY, HIS RUINED **LIFE**, FAR TOO OFTEN NOT TO HOPE FOR IT.

BYE, DAD...

BETTER LUCK NEXT TIME AROUND...

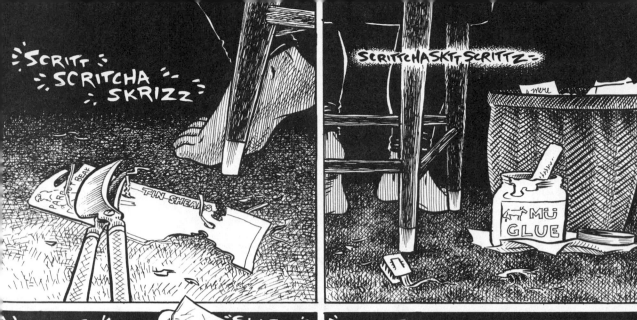

:SCRITT:
:SCRITCHA:
SKRIZZ:

SCRITTCHASKTT SCRITTZ

:SCRIZZITT:
SWIZ
SKRIZ
TZT

:SWIZZA:
C*ZT

:SCRITTCHA SKTTZSWIZZAZIK:
SKITT SCRIZHT SKTT SCRIZZT:
SKRIZZT
SWIZZA
SRIKK
SKRIT
SKTT

IT'S IN MY NATURE TO LOVE CHASING THINGS THAT CAN'T BE CAUGHT.

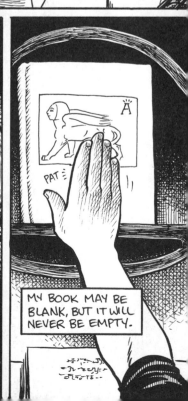

MY BOOK MAY BE BLANK, BUT IT WILL NEVER BE EMPTY.

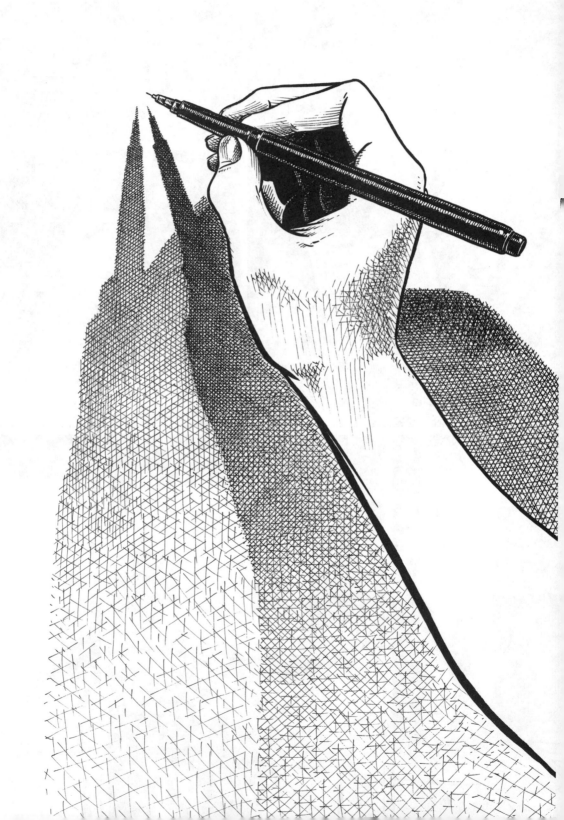

NOTES
ON THE PRECEDING

TITLE PAGE/PAGE V

This is intentionally misquoted. The aphorism appears in *Bartlett's Familiar Quotations* as "My Book and Heart must never Part." The author of this quote is not known.

DEDICATION PAGE/PAGE VII

Drawing based on a little girl I observed in the post office a few days before. Mom was shipping boxes, little sister was hanging on Mom's sweater, and this kid had her nose stuck in one of those Lemony Snicket books. She never looked up from it, trailing after her mother and sister without being called, and without any trouble opening the double doors.

INTRO HEADER/PAGE IX

Lea Hernandez has named the cartoon version of her son which appears in her on-line comic *Near-Life Experience* 'Strangel.' I coined the term while yakking on the phone with her, talking about her son. AS far as I'm concerned, it's our word.

INTRO/PAGE 1

I hadn't come up with an image for this story that really stood out, and I was getting a little nervous about it. The same day I saw the little kid in the post office, I was stuck in heavy traffic behind a car with what must have been two really small kids in the back seat. If one of them hadn't had this silly topknot, I might never have known they were there at all.

All I could see was this little blond ponytail, set high on the crown of her head, held in place by either a really thick rubber band or a really compressed scrunchie. Since I couldn't see the actual kid's head, the effect was of a little puppet head, with a fluffy wig, bobbing about in the rear window.

That night I happened upon a Japanese website for customizable dolls, Their heads come off. The tops of their skulls come off as well, so their owners can a) change the color of their eyes, or the direction at which their eyes are looking, and b) tighten the elastic strings that hold the dolls's bodies together. All kids take their toys apart, and use them in their own inscrutable ways.

PAGE 2

In this world there is a measurable force that is described as magic. The Sylvan clan lay claim to a gift for it, and run well-funded schools to encourage talent for it. They test kids for certain abilities, and award scholarships or special training accordingly.

It's a rather quixotic gift. But that's all you need to know now.

PAGE 3

Ah — Marcie's doll, unlike the ones on that web page, has those strange round eyeballs with eyelids painted on one side. They're weighted so that they 'close' — roll to show the eyelid instead of the eye — when the doll's head is tilted. Many such dolls will 'wink.'

Those odd pegs on the sides of its head are fashion-doll style earrings.

These phrases are excerpted from a C. S. Lewis poem, which appears in my 1960 edition of *Through The Looking-Glass*, but also in the Gutenberg Project on-line:

Child of the pure, unclouded brow
  And dreaming eyes of wonder!
Though time be fleet, and I and thou
  Are half a life asunder,
Thy loving smile will surely hail
  The love-gift of a fairy-tale.

I have not seen thy sunny face
  Nor heard thy silver laughter:
No thought of me shall find a place
  In thy young life's hereafter—
Enough that now thou wilt not fail
  To listen to my fairy-tale.

A tale begun in other days,
  When summer suns were glowing—
A simple chime, that served to time
  The rhythym of our rowing—
Whose echoes live in memory yet,
  Though envious years would say, "forget."

Come, hearken then, ere voice of dread,
  With bitter tidings laden,
Shall summon to unwelcome bed
  A melancholy maiden!
We are but older children, dear,
  Who fret to find our bedtime near.

Without, the frost, the blinding snow,
  The storm-wind's moody madness—
Within, the firelight's ruddy glow,
  And childhood's nest of gladness.
The magic words shall hold thee fast:
  Thou shalt not heed the raving blast.

And, though the shadow of a sigh
  May tremble through the story,
For "happy summer days" gone by,
  And vanish'd summer glory,
It shall not touch, with breath of bale,
  The pleasance of our fairy-tale.

PAGE 7

This is an open market, outside the dome, in what passes for sprawl around the big cities. In this case, however, sprawl doesn't consist of city people who want to live cheaply and own more

FATHER & DAUGHTER, LEJEB CLAN

THIS CLAN DOMINATES MATHEMATICAL BUSINESSES.

land. These city people are convinced that life outside the domes is hazardous. The sprawl-belt is made up of semi-settled people huddled around the trade routes leading into Anvard.

PAGE 8

The animal in the cage is a small quetzal. These flying lizards have feathers and claws on each of their four limbs.

Panel 2. Jaeger has on his belt two dark braids of equal length. These, plus the clocks in the background, are meant to indicate that he's going back to Anvard to check on Emma and her family, as he swore to do at the end of *Sin-Eater*. Jaeger is a trash-picker, a scavenger. He finds things to barter. When he comes back to visit people, he has to bring gifts. This is both his nature and his upbringing.

PAGE 9

The design on the cover of Marcie's gift was based partly on the caduceus and partly on the AURYN symbol in Michael Ende's *The Neverending Story* (a wonderful book and a dreadful movie). AURYN is, in turn, a clear reference to Ouroboros, the world-serpent, and the common symbol of infinity.

Marcie hasn't progressed well in school in part because she was a very sickly kid, and has missed a lot, and partly because her mother is in constant dispute with her grandfather about how the kids should be educated. Granddad, you

HUMM

MARCIE, AGE SIX

see, is Money. Marcie is not of an age to understand this — she just knows that if she expresses no opinion, that Mom and Terry will fight to stalemate and Marcie won't be forced to go to school.

Panel 6. William Goldman says he asked his daughters what kind of story they liked. One said 'princesses,' the other said, 'brides.' So there you have it.

PAGE 10

Quotes: "When suddenly" — Lewis Carroll, *Alice In Wonderland*. "Henceforth" — J. M. Barrie, *Peter Pan*. "My own garden" — Oscar Wilde, *The Selfish Giant*. "It was fourteen" — Stephen King, *Rose Madder*. "The lamb said" — me myself, a mishmosh of Norse and English folktales. "I can't answer" — me myself again. Favorite fantasy stories of mine, all of them.

The figure of Emma and her children on the lower right section comes from a remarkable sculptor, Miles Blackshear. He makes lovely, sentimental resin-figures, beautifully detailed and elegant. This one is from his Ebony Visions line.

PAGE 11

More quotes: "Until" — me again. "Bye, boys!" — William Goldman, *The Princess Bride*. "The bottom" — me. "Awake, awake" — C. S. Lewis, *The Magician's Nephew*. "In order" — Octavia Butler, *The Parable Of The Sower*. "He saw her fall" — me again.

PAGE 12

Cosmic hangover. I live for it.

Panel 3. these tentacular strands emerging from Emma's head are complicated hardware, hookups for her profession. Details aren't really necessary— a lot goes on around Marcie that she doesn't think much about. A whole earthshattering Jaeger Returns scene is taking place all around her, and it's just not making an impression on her.

Panel 3: Mom/ Emma. Panel 4: Older sister Rachel. Panel 5: Older brother Lynne.

PAGE 13

And Dad/Brigham makes his presence known in panel 4. Brigham underwent a number of unpleasant therapies to correct a physical problem, two broken legs; and a psychological problem, an obsessiveness which led to his stalking his wife and family. These therapies don't draw the line between rehabilitation and revenge clearly at all.

PAGE 14

This is, I admit, all rather Gothic, but the influence of the sickly relative on small children is something that fit Marcie well. This Cthulhoid figure lurking in some back bedroom, well, fear is the Philosophers's Stone of the imagination. It transmutes damn near anything into a story.

PAGE 15

Emma's 'tentacles' are connected to these cables. The whole rig makes for a very high-bandwidth connection between Emma's mind and the Pastwatch Institute's recording devices.

PAGE 16

If the thought of people not reading strikes you as implausible — well, it isn't. Literacy isn't really the issue. A staggering number of people who can read don't. Of those who do, many read nothing but magazines, never actual books.

Metus is a merging of the names Medusa and Metis. Their names possibly derive from the same word, which means wisdom or prudence. Mnemo is an abbreviation of Mnemosyne, goddess of memory.

PAGE 17

Top left corner. This is Vince Sneed's character Stella Maris, the Daytripper. She has an enormous sheepdog named Digby. I'm not sure where he means to use them, but they fit.

Panels 2, 3, 4. Panel 2 is Jaeger's retelling of *Night Of The Hunter*, panels 3 and 4 are actual dialogue.

PAGE 18

Panels 4 and 5. Here, Jaeger's kissing his fingers, then transferring the kiss to Marcie's cheek. Dunno if it comes across.

PAGE 19

Oh, the pain! I don't know how many times I just wanted somebody to read to me. Even though I could read— I can't remember a time far back enough that I couldn't— I just wanted to sit in a chair with somebody and have them read to me. But you know almost nobody reads a book well. Sigh.

Rachel's problem is she suffers from smarm. This excess of zeal really doesn't amuse small children. In fact, I have to wonder if it isn't a component of the common fear of clowns. All the adults are smiling — watching you to see what you do — here comes this loud, brightly colored creepazoid, rushing at you, doing weird things. All the signals say that you are supposed to be pleased, encourage you to be excited — what you really want is, perhaps, an elephant gun to fend 'em off with.

PAGES 20 AND 21

This is the kind of incredibly tedious, repetitive writing that characterizes the worst of children's fiction, much of which has never emerged from the Victorian period. This is all fake. In so many ways.

PAGE 22

What's in the book that Rachel flips out over? Probably an illustration. People freak out over visual stuff much more readily than they do over prose.

PAGE 23

'My birthday present.' No, it wasn't really; it wasn't Marcie's birthday. Like Smeagol, she tends to think of her most prized possession as her best present.

PAGE 24

This attitude is not really cruelty. Lynne's way of dealing with Marcie will get her up and out of her slough of despond and into action faster than anything else.

PAGE 25

This school is dominated by Marcie's mother's clan, the Llaveracs. In short, the clans are the ruling classes, they intermarry to an amazing degree, and they all resemble one another fairly closely. Llaveracs are theatrical people, concerned with the arts and with fashion. Their curriculum is not as frivolous as it looks — but it isn't really what suits Marcie. Marcie's father was not Llaverac. Medawars are much earthier, more practical people.

PAGE 26

Marcie disabled and stole one of the roving cameras for Lynne. Lynne's been training her to do this kind of thing since she was able to walk. After all, small kids can smile innocently and get away with murder.

PAGE 27

Bedridden people in nursing homes and 'rest homes' often develop odd behaviors to get attention. Howling is one such. Some just keep up a constant low howl until somebody comes. Most of the howlers won't remember somebody came to check on them five minutes later, so they keep the howling up day and night.

There are kings asleep under hills or mountains in every system of folklore. The king who wakes up and ends the world, that's partly Brahma and partly Alice's Adventures Through The Looking-Glass.

PAGE 28 AND 29

Yes, this is a horrible thing to do to a kid, and yes, it happens every day. I do think books are different, but some kids view the loss of a single

MARCIE, AGE EIGHT

THIS BLACK TURTLENECK-PLUS-TIGHTS THING SHE WEARS IS A COMMON UNIFORM FOR MEDAWAR CHILDREN.

IT'S USED BOTH AS OUTERWEAR AND AS A LINER FOR HEAVIER CLOTHING.

MANY CLANS HAVE UNIFORMS LIKE THIS.

Lego piece is as earthshattering as Marcie views the loss of her book. How's a parent in a heavily-digital society to keep up?

PAGE 33
Now we are in the Midnight Library. Every book is in here, and there will be no fires that destroy. She can barely reach them, but she can read whatever she can pull down.

PAGE 34
Does anybody remember 'the Nothing book'? It was the first blank book I ever saw, way back in the seventies. Its slogan was "Wanna make something of it?"

The importance of this dream is that she's rewarded for taking action. She's given everything she ever wanted, but she has to do something for it. If it was given to her for nothing, it would be nothing.

PAGE 35
Most of her contemporaries simply don't understand why she has all these paper books, or indeed all this paper. It's a hands-on craving. I can't remember anything unless I write it down or draw it. Many of our words for cognition are tactile words. We speak of 'handling' a problem, 'turning it over' in our minds, 'grasping' an idea.

A keyboard just doesn't do it for all of us. The malaise of this age can be terrible. You have nothing, no power, very little independence. Many of us fall under inertia. Marcie can't tolerate boredom — it'll keep her moving.

PAGE 36
Any fourteen-year-old boy who can smoke at the kitchen table in front of his older sister and mother is the ruler of the roost, in nature if not in name.

The small tree growing in the center of the table bears fruits which may be used as condiments.

PAGE 37
Marcie is not me. But this sense of detachment from her feelings, as if they are things that happen to her, that comes from me. Also the ongoing daydream which fends off boredom.

The panel border (and puzzle) comes from Kit Williams' *Masquerade*. More quotes: "You are a little"— Orson Scott Card, *Songmaster*. "I ask for so little"— Jim Henson et al, *Labyrinth*. The Goblin King is one of my favorite not-all-there fantasy figures.

PAGE 38
Quotes: "'Look, everyone'"— Tanith Lee, *The Silver Metal Lover*. "He stared"— William F. Nolan, *Logan's Run*. "There were plenty"— Doris Piserchia, *Spaceling*. "Somehow, it was hotter"— Harper Lee, *To Kill A Mockingbird*. More favorite fantasies.

PAGE 39
Later in her life Marcie was transferred to a school run by and populated with Medawars. Medawars believe in sex-segregation. Llaveracs don't.

Marcie may suffer the slings and arrows of her teachers, who disapprove of her mixed heritage, but Medawar girls are pretty self-willed. Marcie will have friends, even though they think she's bats.

PAGE 40
Marcie's hookup is very simple. Just a crude connection that allows her to manipulate the computer display, receive and transmit simple information, including simple sensations.

PAGE 41
Panel 6 touches briefly on the source of Lynne's fortune, and the focus of his obsession. Many people in this society are forever running after compelling footage to sell to tv and movie companies, such as the one run by Marcie and

Lynne's grandfather. He may be a viciously opportunistic voyeur, but in his society, that's easy money.

PAGE 42
This 'footage' may be seen in *Finder* #11. Any bets on how Lynne got it away from the Huitzi priest who originally shot it?

PAGE 43
There are so many tiny studios... like garage bands, everybody tries to come up with a weird name, anything memorable will do. This would work if they didn't change their names so often.

Panel 4. Lynne shot this image in issue 5, while Jaeger was sleeping in the tub.

PAGE 44
This idea of having direct control of an audience's emotions came from Hitchcock. I shudder to think what would have become of that man if he'd had access to this imaginary technology. Nothing good, I think.

PAGE 45
There are theaters on every other corner in Anvard. They're owned by different 'stations', so going from theater to theater is like changing channels. Of course, most people just stay in their local.

The name of this bookstore is another reference to Michael Ende's *The Neverending Story*. I urge you not to judge that book by its movie.

PAGE 46
The pipe smoke comes from Attic Books, a used-and-rare shop close to me. The owner's got a replica of the Maltese Falcon on his desk. The stuff that dreams are made of.

PAGE 47
I am not Marcie. I didn't have the guts to break the window.

PAGES 48 THROUGH 49
Well... since I can think of nothing to elaborate on these pages, I suppose I might call them successful.

PAGE 50
I had one of these stupid books as a kid. It wasn't cool, though: it was horrible. Big, crude, line-printer type, so obviously fake. It was illustrated with classic images from Maurice Sendak, Dr. Seuss, all the greats — badly reprinted, entirely without context, and almost certainly used without permission. The story left no impression on me whatever, but the

MARCIE TAKES AFTER HER MEDAWAR FATHER, EXCEPT FOR HER HAIR (WHICH ISN'T TURNING DARK BROWN WITH MATURITY) AND HER NEARSIGHTEDNESS (COMMON AMONG HER MOTHER'S CLAN).

surrealism of these familiar pictures thrown in for no reason both appealed to and appalled me. I have no idea where that book went. No doubt my mother threw it out.

One other thing. I did to one of my small cousins what Jaeger did to Marcie. Y'know how a kid will bring you the same book over and over and over again. They just want to sit with you, more than anything else. Fine for the kid — death for the adult. So I would just make stuff up. I'd blather and she'd turn the pages whenever she felt like it, and I'd just blabber on until she decided the book was over. I don't know if she really knew I wasn't reading, but she always brought me that same book, and wouldn't ask anyone else to read that particular one. I used to worry about what would happen when she got old enough to learn to read. I needn't have worried. She's ten now, and has no recollection of my doing this at all.

PAGE 51
Lynne's a good Vulcan. Vulcan thinking cuts through a lot of troublesome melodrama.

PAGE 57
Now I've got people pestering me to write the story Marcie's writing. I can barely keep track of

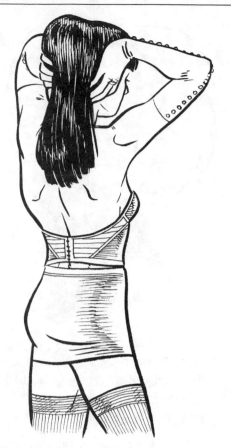

what goes on in my own head! How can I know more about what goes on in hers?

The three small panels are meant to look like sticky-notes. This is what my notebooks look like— messes of sketches and gibberish covered with phone numbers and sticky-notes.

On the sticky-notes: such things as 'martinene 144-bv-273' are 'namebers'. That's a phone ID number that follows you wherever you go. It's not always a bad idea, except when it's a terrible idea.

PAGE 58

This bookstore scene is taken directly from life, with me as Marcie. Poor kid! I knew just how she felt. When you're that age, you lose track of The Right Book easily— you don't remember titles or think to write down authors' names. I loved this one odd little book when I was in the third grade, had no idea what it was called or who wrote it (wrote it?? Nobody WROTE it! It's just, y'know, like, a BOOK I like!), and couldn't find it again. Not until I was twenty-six years old did I spot it again— riding under the elbow of a customer in the bookstore I was working in. I pounced on her, I can tell you; I'd recognized the cover and I HAD to have a better look at it.

Thank God, she understood completely. She was One Of Us, fellow book freak. *No Flying In The House* by Betty Brock, wonderfully illustrated by Wallace Tripp. I felt so strongly about that book when I was seven, I rewrote the ending on the two blank pages at the back of the book. In grubby pencil. That little hardcover may still be out there, with my first attempt at script-doctoring pencilled in. Who can say?

PAGE 59

Smoko the Magnificent and his Lovely Assistant are both members of Sylvan clan. Sylvans have odd talents for what they call magic. This is smoke sculpture, a mostly useless form of psychokinesis. Smoke particles drifting in the air are easy to manipulate.

Many of the references — light making a statue blink, the library book — these are references to a Studio Ghibli movie called Whisper Of The Heart. Japanese anime. A beautifully-plotted exercise in serendipity and 'real' magic. If you can get past the John Denver song that serves as a theme, it's amazing.

PAGE 60

"Scepticism is the chastity of the intellect, and it is shameful to surrender it too soon or to the first comer: there is nobility in preserving it coolly and proudly throught long youth, until at last, in the ripeness of instinct and discretion, it can be safely exchanged for fidelity and happiness." George Santayana, *Scepticism and Animal Faith, IX*.

Why is Lynne, of all people, applying lipstick? Over a five-o-clock shadow? Well... he's a complicated person. He imagines this is something Jaeger would never do in a million years.

PAGE 61

Marcie's Medawar side comes out. Medawars are really solid, practical, rolled-up-sleeves kind of people. If she can't have 'magic', which, since it exists on a shaky foundation of mood, must be delicately danced around, she'll pitch in and learn the hands-on stuff.

PAGE 62

See? Screech-owl. I'd had this job in mind for her for a long time. Marcella Grosvenor, queen of the Silver Scream. The kind of person who's just a footnote on movie history, known only to serious collectors of trivia.

PAGE 63

Panel 3. Yes, the lady in leopard-skins is actually Marcie's grandfather, Terry Ellis Lockhart. Llaveracs love female fashion, in clothing and in skin.

PAGE 64

"Daughter-of-war" is a literal translation of 'Marcella,' Marcie's full name.

A tarn is an alpine lake formed by glaciation. They're usually round. Bronze-age people would throw in weapons, jewelry, bones, bodies, whatever tribute or libation seemed fitting. Like fountains in malls, I suppose; people can't resist throwing in a penny and making a wish.

Yes, okay, fine; the warrior-goddess at the deep end of the pool did come from youthful late-night viewings of *Heavy Metal* on HBO. So kill me.

PAGE 66

This armor is fetishistic and rather impractical, but hey, it's her fantasy. Let the kid have some fun.

PAGE 67

Note that Marcie has removed her glasses for her bounce down these dark stairs. For those who are not near-sighted, this increases a feeling of... dissociation, a sensation of floating. You can't quite see where you're going, so you'd better know the territory intimately.

Panel 3. This frustration — mood broken, story gone — was described by a pen-pal as the GODDAMNFUCKSHITS. Yep. That's basically it. It's the bitch-slap of the muse.

PAGE 68

Go read *The Color Of Light* by William Goldman. Then I'll discuss this page.

PAGE 69

That hideous drawing is one of mine, circa age five. No, you may not look at it. Ever.

Panel 7. this is a teenaged Medawar orderly. They don't all become full-fledged doctors or nurses, but they all receive a lot of medical training. They're all expected to learn from their mistakes. This girl made a pretty dumb mistake

PAGE 70

Then the Medawar girl compounded it by freaking out. She could easily have done what Marcie does to get Brigham off of her. She'll have quite a lecture waiting for her when she has to explain the condition of her arm back at the hospital.

PAGE 72

The sphinxes come from *The Neverending Story*, and from the New York Public Library (since I couldn't use their lovely lions). The Palace Of Memory is *not* a public library. It's the private property of a very aristocratic family, the Ambersons, whose name is a tribute to Orson Welles.

PAGE 73

Practicality and fantasy fistfight in Heaven. You can't do good work without making a balance between them. Not a balance so much as an engine.

PAGE 73

Bottom left — an e-book is a file. That object is an eBook Reader™ (as well as a day planner and heaven knows what all). It happens to come with new books already loaded. On the bottom right are the small chips containing more books that can be loaded into the reader.

The object in panel 2 is a cardboard dust jacket for an eBook Reader™, originally designed to protect such things from scratches, but sold in the zillions as accessories.

PAGES 74 THROUGH 75

Okay, yes, I actually did this. I blew a *day* doing this. But mine was still there when I went back for it.

PAGE 77

The cut-open-to-reveal-deeper-self also comes from *The Voyage of the Dawn Treader*. Inside the dragon-thing is Marcie's looney Cthulhoid father. Inside the looney father is Brigham back when he wasn't apparently looney. When you can't really have him back... he's worse than the dragon.

PAGE 78

He quiets when she picks him up. Just as he used to do when she was the child.

PAGE 79

Yes, my book is still empty.

PAGE 80

I have two lamps in my studio. I see this double shadow when I work. The idea of using this image, the moment before creation, came directly from Oscar in Dave Sim's *Jaka's Story*.

cover gallery

finder #19 (september 2000)

finder #20 (november 2000)

finder #21 (march 2001)

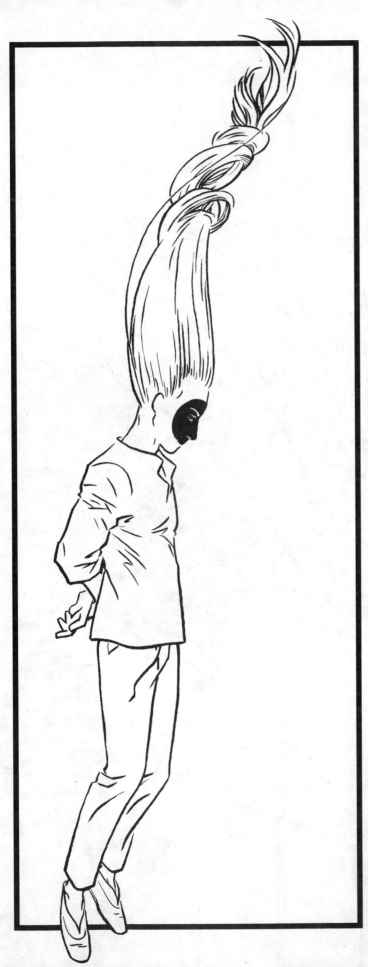

also by carla speed mcneil...

finder: sin-eater, part one tpb
Volume One collects issues 1
through 7, along with relevant
footnotes, a portrait gallery, and a
beautiful new painted cover!
$17.95 U.S. 0-9673691-0-X

finder: sin-eater, part two tpb
Volume Two collects issues 8
through 14, the usual footnotes, a
gallery of never-before-seen artwork
by the artist and friends, and a
spanking-new 8 page story, available nowhere else!
$19.95 U.S. 0-9673691-1-8

finder: king of the cats tpb
FINDER Volume 3 collects issues 15
through 18, plus illustrated footnotes, a new prologue and covers.
$13.95 0-9673691-2-6

mystery date bagged set
The Mystery Date Companion is a
bagged set containing both issues,
an ashcan of the original
Mythography short stories, and an
invaluable footnote booklet.
$8.00 U.S.

original artwork
from FINDER tpb Volumes One and
Two are available for purchase.

finder: the series
Finder continues in 2002 with
Dream Sequence, beginning with
issue #23.

need more information?
LIGHTSPEED PRESS
P.O. Box 448
Annapolis Junction, MD
20701

speed@lightspeedpress.com

www.lightspeedpress.com